For the children and staff at
West Earlham Infant and Nursery School,
who are definitely NOT naughty ninjas! DB

For Jane. Ta very much for keeping the faith.
We did it! BM

SIMON AND SCHUSTER

First published in Great Britain in 2016 by Simon and Schuster UK Ltd • 1st Floor, 222 Gray's Inn Road, London, WC1X 8HB • A CBS Company

Text copyright © 2016 David Bedford • Illustrations copyright © 2016 Becka Moor

The right of David Bedford and Becka Moor to be identified as the author and illustrator of this work has been asserted by them in accordance with the Copyright, Designs and Patents Act, 1988 • All rights reserved, including the right of reproduction in whole or in part in any form

A CIP catalogue record for this book is available from the British Library upon request

ISBN: 978-1-4711-2191-3 (PB) • ISBN: 978-1-4711-2192-0 (ebook) • Printed in Italy • 10 9 8 7 6 5 4

THE THREE NINJA PIGS

DAVID BEDFORD AND BECKA MOOR

London   New Delhi

Once upon a time there were three little pigs . . .

Lemonade and Balloons

VACANCY!
Balloon Blower-Upper
Only those with enough
HUFF'N'PUFF need apply

OOPS! This isn't **THAT** story.

Once upon a time there were . . .

'You **NAUGHT**y ninjas,' said Mrs Pig.
'You've broken yet another cup!
Now *I* need a break!

Off you go to Granny's.

AND NO . . .

MORE . . .

TROUBLE!'

Down the road and through
the woods went the
Three Ninja Pigs,

ALL the way to Granny's cottage.

HEE-YA   HEE-YA   HEE-YA

But when they got there they couldn't believe their eyes.

'Is that you, Granny?' said the worried little ninjas.

'You **NAUGH**ty ninjas! What have you done?'
said Granny, when she came in from chatting
to Little Red Riding Hood.

'Now take this lunch to your Uncle Sam,

AND NO . . . MORE . . . TROUBLE.'

Down the lane and over the
bridge went the Three Ninja Pigs,
all the way to Uncle Sam's building yard.

BUILDER'S YARD
THIS WAY

But when they got there they couldn't believe their eyes.

'ME AGAIN!'
said the big bad wolf.

'I'LL SMASH!'

'AND I'LL KNOCK THIS ALL DOWN!'

'Not by the hair on our chinny chin chins!' said the ninjas.

'AND I'LL CRASH!'

But it was too late.

With a

HUFF!

and a

PUFF!

the wolf was gone.

'You **NAUGHTY** ninjas!' said Uncle Sam.

'My porridge was just right, but this mess is **ALL WRONG!**
Now, off you go and take this shelf to Cindy's boutique.

AND NO . . . MORE . . . TROUBLE.'

PINOCCHIO'S

EMPEROR'S

BACK IN
5 MINS

Down the high street and round the corner
went the Three Ninja Pigs.
But when they got to Cindy's boutique . . .

. . . they couldn't believe their eyes!

'WHAT NOW?'
they cried.

'GUESS WHO?!'

said the big bad wolf.

'MY MUM CAN MARRY A PRINCE IN THESE GLASS SLIPPERS!'

'Only if they fit!'

'AND I'D LIKE TO SEE A FAIRY GODMOTHER GET YOU OUT OF THAT!'

'I'M MAKING **YOU** AN UGLY SISTER!'
laughed the wolf.

'AND **YOU** THE OTHER ONE.
HA HA HA!'

Then

'STOP!'

DING!

DONG!

BONG!

The clock struck twelve
and the wolf was gone.

'Oh, you **NAUGHT**y ninjas!' wailed Cindy,
when she **FINALLY** came out from the changing rooms.

'I'll be late for my date with Prince Charming!
Now take these ribbons to Auntie Rapunzel's hair salon.

AND NO . . . MORE . . . TROUBLE.'

The Three Ninja Pigs decided
it was time for a **SECRET NINJA MEETING!**

WHISPER

WHISPER

WHISPER

SSHHHHH!

Then they snuck and *slid,*
and CROUCHED

and **hid,**

until . . .

And they *styled* and *piled*

and **glued**

and **glossed**

until . . .

'OH HUFF!' said the wolf.

'What a naughty, NAUGHTY wolf!'
said Mrs Pig. 'I know JUST
the place for you!

Sit there quietly . . .

AND NO MORE
TROUBLE.'